DEAR FRIENDS,

A Rack Railw... ...called Culdee
Fell. Lord Harry ... ...s Chairman of the Railway
Company. Lots of people travel on it in the summer.

Mr Walter Richards, the Manager, does not have an
easy time. There are seven engines, one of whom, No. 5,
is still away being mended. Another, No. 6, was named
Lord Harry. This was a mistake. It made him conceited
and . . . But you must read the stories for yourselves.

I hope you will enjoy this book about a different
kind of railway.

THE AUTHOR

The author gratefully acknowledges the help cheerfully and willingly given by members of management and staff of the Snowdon Mountain Railway Ltd, in the preparation of this book.

Mountain Engine

Sir Handel had had a bad day. The old coaches, Agnes, Ruth, Lucy, Jemima and Beatrice, had been "awkward". They had made him slip to a standstill twice. He was furious.

"Those cattle-trucks should be scrapped," he fumed.

Skarloey was shocked. "I won't have it," he protested. "Those old dears need kindness, not bad names."

"Exactly so," agreed Rheneas. He winked at Skarloey. "You be thankful, Sir Handel, that we're not a mountain railway."

"A mountain railway! What's that?"

Titles in this series

Railway Series, No. 19

MOUNTAIN ENGINES

by
THE REV. W. AWDRY

with illustrations by

GUNVOR & PETER EDWARDS

EGMONT

EGMONT

We bring stories to life

First published in Great Britain in 1964
This edition published 2011
by Egmont UK Limited
239 Kensington High Street, London W8 6SA

Thomas the Tank Engine & Friends™

CREATED BY BRITT ALLCROFT

Based on The Railway Series by The Reverend W Awdry
© 2011 Gullane (Thomas) LLC A HiT Entertainment company.

Thomas the Tank Engine & Friends and Thomas & Friends are trademarks of Gullane (Thomas) Limited
Thomas the Tank Engine & Friends and Design is Reg. U.S. Pat. & Tm. Off.

HiT entertainment

ISBN 978 1 4052 0349 4

1 3 5 7 9 10 8 6 4 2

Printed and bound in China

"A railway which climbs mountains, of course."

"But it can't," said Sir Handel. "Its engines' wheels would slip!"

"But it can," said Rheneas firmly. "We've heard of one quite near here."

"It can't."

"It can."

A noisy argument started just as Donald shunted a flat truck to the siding nearby. On the truck was a queer-looking engine. He had six small wheels and a stove-pipe chimney. His boiler was tilted downwards, and his cylinders were "back to front".

'Wheesht!" whispered Donald hoarsely. "Dinna wake the wee engine. It's tired he is. He's away back from England after being mended. Ye ken how it is."

"We understand; but who is he?"

"He's called Culdee, after the mountain his railway climbs."

"Well! Did you ever . . . !" exclaimed the two old engines. They looked at Sir Handel and chuckled.

"I don't believe it!" said Sir Handel.

"Och, ye'd best ask him yeself. Then maybe ye'll learn it's the truth I've been telling ye."

Donald puffed away, offended.

Culdee woke to find the engines gazing at him. "Where am I?" he asked.

They told him. "That's good," he said. "I'm nearly home now."

"Do you really climb mountains?" asked Skarloey.

"I've done it for years."

"You *must* be clever. We couldn't. Our wheels would slip."

"I'm not really clever," laughed Culdee. "I was just drawn like that."

"Like what?"

"With pinion wheels on my driving axles. They have teeth, you see, which fit into a rack rail. I can't slip, however steep the line is."

"That," said Rheneas, "must help you going up; but if your line is so steep, aren't you frightened coming down?"

"Why? We have good brakes."

"Coaches," went on Rheneas, "are sometimes silly and try to push us downhill. Some . . . hrm . . . engines find it hard to stop them."

Sir Handel blushed and looked at his buffers.

"Our coaches," answered Culdee, "are never silly like that. They know such tricks are dangerous. I've never had that sort of accident. But," he went on thoughtfully, "I was frightened once – very frightened indeed."

"Please tell us," said all the engines.

"One day, long ago, before our line was opened, our Drivers made all five of us engines stand ready outside our shed. 'The Inspector's coming,' they said. 'We don't know which of you he'll choose.'

"He chose me, climbed into my cab, and made me push two coaches to the Summit.

"'So far, so good,' he said. 'Now, we'll test your brakes.'

"So he went and stood on the steepest part of the line. Down, down it fell, with a nasty curve below, edging a precipice.

"'Brakes off, Driver. Let him roll.'"

"Oooh!" gasped the little engines in horror.

"The coaches nudged me. We gathered speed downhill. I was terrified . . .

"My Driver's hand stole to the brake. 'Hands off,' ordered the Inspector.

"Then I remembered I had automatic brakes. I could put these on myself. Perhaps the Inspector wanted to see if I could. They worked beautifully.

"'Well done, Culdee,' said the Inspector. 'You'll do!'

"I smiled, of course, but felt *very* shaky. My Driver and Fireman mopped their faces. They'd been nervous too!

"I'm never nervous now," finished Culdee. "Why should I be? There's no need."

Bad Look-out

R HENEAS and Skarloey were talking quietly to Culdee next morning when Duncan stormed up, followed by Sir Handel.

"Hullo," chuckled Rheneas, "here we go!"

"I nearly came off," fumed Duncan. "Those coaches *pushed* me. The Thin Controller says they didn't. He says I kept a Bad Look-out.

" 'We've no money to mend you,' he said, 'and if it happens again I'll leave you at the back of the Shed.' Why does he always pick on me? It's not fair . . ."

Skarloey said nothing. He just winked at Rheneas like this.

18

"As you were saying, Culdee," remarked Rheneas. "You had two coaches on your trial trip. Do you ever take more?"

"No; our line is so steep that we're only allowed one. We each have our own. Mine's called Catherine. I know her well. That's most important."

"Why?" asked Sir Handel. "They're only coaches."

"Ours," said Culdee, "are something more. You pull your coaches, and you can see ahead. We *push* ours up, so we can't see. They watch the line for us. The Guard watches too, of course, but Catherine's so clever that I know at once if anything is wrong."

"That must take a load off your mind," said Skarloey.

Culdee smiled. "But not off my buffers! Climbing's hard work, and needs a lot of steam. My Fireman and I have a tiring time. Coming down," he went on, "it's different. Catherine and I just roll. We need no steam for that."

Sir Handel sighed enviously. "I should like that," he said. "With your automatic brakes, it sounds like a Rest Cure."

"That," replied Culdee, "was just the mistake poor Godred made!"

"Who," asked the little engines, "is Godred?"

"Godred *was* our No. 1, and named after a king," Culdee replied. "Perhaps that went to his smokebox and made him conceited. He'd never keep a Good Look-out. He'd roll down the line looking anywhere but at the track.

"'You'll have an accident,' I told him.

"'Pooh!' he said. 'I've got automatic brakes, haven't I? And Driver's got his air brake. What more do you want?'

"'More sense from you,' I said. 'No engine can stop at once if he isn't ready to obey his Driver's controls.' "

"The first thing a young engine learns," agreed Skarloey.

"Godred never learnt sense. His Driver and Fireman and the Manager all spoke to him. They even took him to pieces to see if anything was wrong; but he still went on in the same old way.

"One day I was going up, and waited at a station for Godred, coming down, to pass me. As I waited, so it happened. One moment he was on the track; the next, his Driver and Fireman jumped clear as he rolled over.

"No one was hurt. His coach stayed on the rails, and the Guard braked her to a stop.

"They brought Godred home next day.

"'We've no money to mend you,' said our Manager, 'so you'll go to the back of the Shed!'

"As time went on, poor Godred got smaller and smaller till nothing was left."

"Wha . . . what happened?" asked Duncan anxiously.

"It's not nice to talk about," said Culdee.

"But what *happened*? Why isn't it nice?"

"Our Drivers used Godred's parts to mend us," answered Culdee mournfully.

Sir Handel and Duncan were unusually silent long after Culdee had gone home.

Neither Skarloey nor Rheneas ever mentioned that Culdee had made the story up.

Danger Points

DONALD brought Culdee up the valley to the exchange-siding, where he was soon off-loaded by crane.

His Driver and Fireman and the Manager were there. They all said "Goodbye" and "Thank you" to Donald. Then they lit Culdee's fire, and while waiting for the steam, they looked him over carefully.

"A very good job," they said at last.

Culdee sizzled happily. "It's lovely to be at home and in steam again," he said. "I'm longing to have a run with Catherine."

"Come on then," said his Driver, and they trundled to the Shed.

Catherine was pleased to see him, and they went for a short run. "I've had to go with Lord Harry lately," she said. "He takes risks and frightens me. When I warn him, he laughs."

"Never mind," comforted Culdee. "It'll be all right now."

Later, he met two old friends, Ernest (No. 2), and Wilfred (No. 3). After some happy gossip, Culdee asked, "Who is Lord Harry?"

"He's one of the new engines," they said, "who came while you were away. He's No. 6; Alaric and Eric are 7 and 8. They're nice quiet engines, but old Harry's a 'terror'."

Next afternoon, Lord Harry rolled by with a reluctant coach, on his way to the platform.

"Stupid things," he grumbled. "They're all scared of coming with me."

"You're too reckless," said Culdee. "That's why."

"Rubbish! I'm up-to-date, that's all. I can go twice your speed in perfect safety."

"All the same, we don't take such risks on mountain railways."

"There's no risk. Why, with my superheat . . ."

"Oh!" interrupted Culdee, "it's superheat, is it? I'd have said it was conceit, myself." Lord Harry snorted furiously away.

"Ooooh!" screamed the coach as her wheels ground on the curves. "Be careful!"

"Pooh!" snorted Lord Harry. "I like things to be exciting."

Every wise mountain engine knows that you do not take risks, and that points *must* be taken slowly; for there, the rack rail can have no Guards.

"Steady boy! Steady!" warned his Driver; but Lord Harry paid no attention. He was thinking what he'd say to Culdee next time they met. "There's no danger," he boasted, storming up the final slope. "That patched-up old ruin was talking nonsense."

The telephone rang in the Shed, and Culdee's crew were joined by the Manager. "Lord Harry's 'off' at the Summit," he said. "We shall have to go and put things right."

So they collected some workmen and the tool-van, and set out at once.

It was getting dark when they arrived. Lord Harry's shape loomed against the sky. He had come off at the points and blocked both roads of the station. Wilfred was there with his coach, unable to start his journey down. The passengers buzzed round Lord Harry like angry bees. He was feeling harassed!

The Manager pacified the passengers, while Culdee buffered up behind to take the strain when the men levered the engine's front wheels on to the rails.

"Wilfred," he called, "who is this wreck?"

"It's Lord Harry; didn't you know?"

"It looks like Old Harry; it's fat as Old Harry, but of course it can't be Old Harry."

"Why ever not?"

"You see, Old Harry's an up-to-date engine. He can go twice our speed in perfect safety."

"Tee hee hee!" tittered the coaches.

Lord Harry seethed in silence.

They pushed Lord Harry out of the way, and took the passengers home. Then Culdee helped him back to the Shed.

"It was that coach, Sir," blustered Lord Harry. "She never . . ."

"No tales," said the Manager sharply. "It was your fault, and you know it. You upset our passengers and damaged yourself by taking risks. We cannot have that on our Mountain Railway."

"But, Sir . . ."

"That's enough. You will stay in the Shed till we have decided what to do with you."

He turned, and walked sternly away.

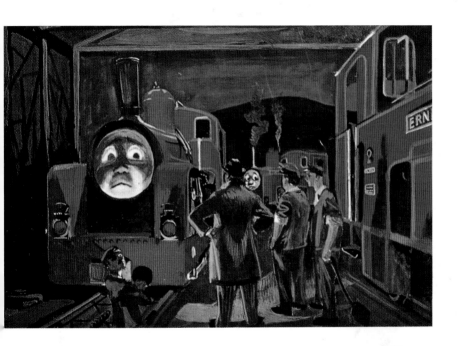

"Devil's Back"

As a punishment, they took Lord Harry's name away, and put him at the back of the Shed. He soon heard Culdee's story about Godred.

"Pooh!" he said. "That couldn't happen to me." But he was anxious all the same.

"Please, Sir, I'm sorry. I'll try to be different."

"The passengers don't trust you," said the Manager. "You will take the 'Truck' instead."

So No. 6 took supplies to Summit Hotel, and he took gangers to work in the morning and brought them home in the evening. He found it dull, and grumbled.

"It's important work," protested Wilfred, "and tough, too."

"Tough! That little lot?"

"Yes, tough," said Culdee. "Have you ever been across Devil's Back in a gale?"

"No," said No. 6 thoughtfully, "but I see what you mean."

A mile below Summit, the line runs along a rocky ridge. Always there is wind. Sometimes it is gentle; at others it is fierce and very dangerous. Then all passenger trains stop at Devil's Back Station, but whatever the weather, stores trains and rescue trains *must* get through.

A few days later, No. 6 reached Devil's Back at 5.15. he was on his way, with the Truck, to fetch railway staff from Summit.

"All clear now," said the Stationmaster, as the last "down" train left the loop. "Don't waste time. The wind's rising. We'll have a gale in half an hour."

He went inside to set the points, but the telephone rang and he came out looking worried. "There's trouble," he told the crew. "Come in and discuss it out of the wind."

They filled the Truck's big tank with water, and sandbags ballasted the van. The wind whistled round them as they worked.

"What is all this?" asked No. 6.

"There's been a climbing accident," explained his Driver. "Culdee and Catherine are bringing up a Doctor and a Rescue Team, but Catherine's too light to stand this gale, so we'll go up ourselves. The water and the sandbags will steady us if you can keep going, we have a good chance of getting through. Can you do it?"

"I'll have a jolly good try," said No. 6.

When Culdee arrived, the Doctor and the Rescue Team changed trains. The Manager was there too. "Splendid!" he said, when he saw the preparations. "Now, No. 6, it's up to you."

The Guard signalled the Driver, and they were off.

"A real job at last," crowed No. 6 exultantly. "Now I'll show them! Now I'll show them . . ." Leaving the shelter of the station, the full force of the gale struck him like a blow.

Culdee and Catherine saw him waver. "Go it! Go it!" they yelled.

No. 6 heard them for a moment; the next, he was battling on alone.

He didn't feel so brave now. All he wanted was to get out of the vicious, stinging, icy wind which seemed to come at him from all directions.

The Truck lurched and swayed as the wind tore at it. It whimpered and groaned as though in pain.

"She wants to go back," thought No. 6. "And so do I; but we can't. The Manager's relying on me to save those climbers. We must go through – we must! We must!"

Slowly, doggedly he struggled on, till in shelter, again on the other side, they climbed the final steep ascent, and rolled triumphant into Summit Station.

They brought the climbers safely down, and an ambulance whisked them to hospital. Next morning, their leader came to say "Thank you".

"My friend Patrick," he said, "hurt himself helping me, but he's mending now, thanks to you and your brave engine. We'd all be proud if you'd call him Patrick, too."

The Manager smiled. "Well, No. 6, would you like that?" he asked?

"Oh, Sir! Yes, please."

Patrick and the others are all good friends. He is still brave, still ready to take risks when needed, but he knows now that it is stupid to take them just for the sake of showing off!